# Guests Deserve the Best

## by Menucha Fuchs

adapted by Shoshana Lepon

illustrated by Estie Hass

Guests have come to visit
And everybody knows
That guests deserve the very best.
That's how the mitzvah goes.

But in the kitchen fridge
Things are just not right.
Something strange is in the back.
It's orange, big and bright.

3

Abba looks in and opens his eyes,
"What can that be?" he says in surprise.
"I'm looking for some yummy plums,
'Cause fruit is always great."
He finds the plums in the bottom bin
And puts them on a plate.

5

Then Chani opens up the fridge
And looks inside, as well.
"What can I give our guests to eat?
Peaches would be swell!"

She sees something orange in the back.
It's too big for a peach.
She finds the peaches near the milk
Just within her reach.

Yaakov comes to the kitchen next
For oranges, bright and sweet.
He looks around inside the fridge
But all he finds is meat.

"What's that big thing in the back?
I've never seen a fruit so big."
He finds the oranges under the beets.
All he had to do was dig!

9

Now Rachel looks for something special
That she can give the guests.
"How about some tasty melon?
My treat will be the best!"

There's something orange, large and round,
But a melon it can't be.
Oh! There's the melon, right below,
Right next to the iced tea.

Then Ima comes in, opens the fridge,
And pulls out a big pot.
"I made our guests some creamy soup.
It's sure to hit the spot!"

"But what is that?" she thinks aloud,
Looking in, surprised.
"I never bought anything so big.
I can't believe my eyes!"

13

And that's when little Shimi comes over.

14

15

16

"Guests deserve the
    best," he laughs,
"And so I saved my
    treat for last!
Better than the sweetest fruit,
Better than the finest soup..."

17

He pulls out a big, round, orange balloon
For the children to play with
     in the living room.

"I wanted to keep my
     treat from popping,
So I kept it safe in here!"

Then Shimi gives
the guests his treat,
And everybody cheer

19

# Every Kid Deserves A Little *Menucha!*

## The Menucha V'Simcha Series

The Flying B___ · by Menucha ___ · illustrated by ___

The Puppe___ · by Menucha ___ · illustrated by ___

The Most Be___ Picture in the ___ · by Menucha ___ · illustrated by ___

Hide and G___ · by Menucha ___ · adapted by ___ · illustrated by ___

The Little ___ · by Menucha ___ · adapted by ___ · illustrated by ___

The Best Gift · by Menucha Fu___ · adapted by ___ · illustrated by ___

Just A Pinch · by Menucha Fuchs · adapted by Simchone Leopen · illustrated by Estie Ho___

## The Sipur V'Sefer Series

Menucha Fuchs — **Donny Duckling Finds a Friend**

Menucha Fuchs — **Now Dovy Bear ___**

**Gavriel and the Golden Garden** — Menucha Fuchs

Menucha Fuchs — **Who Will Be King of the Jungle?**

## The Children's Learning Series

CHILDREN'S STORIES ABOUT **CHESSED** · BY MENUCHA FUCHS · ILLUSTRATED BY ___

**MIDDOS** STORIES FOR CHILDREN

CHILDREN'S STORIES ABOUT **FRIENDSHIP**

**PESACH** WITH THE COHEN FAMILY · BY MENUCHA FUCHS · ILLUSTRATED BY CHAYA

**A PURIM CELEBRATION** AND OTHER PURIM STORIES · BY MENUCHA FUCHS · ILLUSTRATED BY ___

**20 books in this popular series!**